Sandy's Story

D1297206

Penguin Group (USA) LLC
375 Hudson Street
New York, New York 10014

USA * Canada * UK * Ireland * Australia
New Zealand * India * South Africa * China

penguin.com
A Penguin Random House Company

First published in the United States of America by Puffin Books,
an imprint of Penguin Young Readers Group, 2014

CIP data is available.

PB ISBN: 978-0-14-751213-0 / HC ISBN: 978-0-14-751214-7

Printed in the United States of America

1 3 5 7 9 10 8 6 4 2

Inspired by the hit Broadway musical

Annie®

Sandy's Story

Written by Ashley Fedor

based on the original novel by Thomas Meehan

PUFFIN BOOKS
An Imprint of Penguin Group (USA)

Chapter One

Many years ago, on the Lower East Side of Manhattan in a tiny tenement apartment building, there lived a dog and his family, the Moores. Mr. Moore sold vegetables from a pushcart, Mrs. Moore was a washerwoman, and although their four children were always running between school and odd jobs around the neighborhood, the kids always found time to play with their beloved dog, whom they named Sammy after Uncle Sam. "Papa says that Uncle Sam stands for the United States. We're going to have a better life here than we had in Ireland," the oldest daughter, Kathleen, told Sammy as she brushed his shaggy brown hair. Sammy loved Kathleen the best of all. She had long, wavy red hair, and she always brought him an extra bone when she returned home from buying the family's Sunday roast at the butcher shop. And although Mr. Moore told the children that Sammy needed to sleep in the courtyard of their tenement building, sometimes Kathleen would sneak him inside after her parents had gone to bed. "You're my best friend, Sammy," she would whisper as they snuggled in the cramped bedroom that all four kids shared.

Sammy liked to play with the younger kids—the little twins, Michael and Matthew, and middle sister, Bridget—but he was the most loyal to Kathleen. She was kind and loving, and though the food on the table seemed to be getting scarcer and scarcer, Kathleen would always slip him some of her dinner. Sammy loved mealtimes, especially when he got scraps of meat followed by a scratch behind the ears. But after a while, there was no more meat on Sundays, and no more bones for Sammy. Then Kathleen seemed to hardly ever be around.

"I took a job washing dishes at the restaurant downstairs," she told Sammy one night. "Mama and Papa say that they thought things would get better, but it's been three years since the stock market crash and everyone is still poor." She sighed. "I had to drop out of school, too, so I can spend more time working." Sammy didn't quite understand, but it made him sad to see Kathleen so unhappy. Seeing the tears streaming from her eyes, Sammy jumped in her lap and licked at her face. Kathleen giggled. "As long as I have you, Sammy, I don't care how poor we are!"

Sammy didn't care much about being poor,

either. Scraps from the table, a warm place to sleep, and Kathleen were all he needed.

But one day, after a long afternoon of chasing sticks with the twins, Sammy came in to find Mr. and Mrs. Moore hurriedly packing things into boxes while Kathleen scrubbed the kitchen.

"Mama, what's going on?" Michael asked worriedly. Mrs. Moore looked up sadly and took the twins aside, speaking to them in a low voice. Kathleen rushed over to Sammy.

"Papa says we have to leave New York," she cried into his fur. "There's just no money anymore. Mama hasn't had any customers in weeks—everyone is washing their own clothes now—and Papa can't make enough at the vegetable cart. We're moving to California to live with Mama's brother. He's going to get Papa a job."

California! Sammy wagged his tail. The shaggy dog had never heard of California, but it sounded far away and fun. So why was Kathleen crying? He looked up at his red-headed friend.

Kathleen sniffled and hugged Sammy tighter. "The worst part is that we have to leave you, Sammy. Mama and Papa say it's too far to take a dog."

Leave me? Sammy didn't understand. How could Kathleen leave him? Where would he go? Who would take care of him?

"Maybe we'll come back to New York someday," Kathleen told the dog, though she didn't sound certain.

For the rest of the evening, Sammy watched sadly as his family packed all their belongings into boxes and bags. That night, Mr. and Mrs. Moore let him stay in the children's room—but Sammy couldn't sleep. He spent the night wide awake, tucked under Kathleen's arm, worrying about what he would do when the Moores left the next day. And in the morning, after Sammy took one last walk with the kids, Kathleen knelt down in the alley and threw her arms around her dog. "I'll miss you so much, Sammy," she sobbed. "But I know you'll find someone who will love you as much as I do."

I hope so, thought Sammy sadly.

"Kathleen! It's time for us to go!" called Mrs. Moore.

Kathleen unwrapped her handkerchief and dropped its contents on the ground—a small boiled potato, her whole breakfast. "I'll never forget you, my best puppy dog," she said tearfully, and then she was gone. Sammy was left alone.

Chapter Two

Life wasn't easy for a stray dog on the streets of New York City in 1933, especially in the winter. Sammy had been with the Moores since he was a puppy, and he didn't really know how to fend for himself. He wandered through the alleys, desperately searching for food and cover from the rain and snow. On his first day in the streets, Sammy spotted another dog—a black-and-white mutt—sprinting down Delancey Street. Before he could decide whether to follow the dog, a boy of about nine or ten came running after the pup. Grabbing the black-and-white dog by the collar, the boy said, out of breath, "Spot! Never run away from me again. What would happen if a policeman caught you? You'd go straight to the dog pound and I'd never see you again, that's what. Now we'd better get along home."

Sammy didn't know what a dog pound was, but it didn't sound good. *I'd better watch out for policemen, then,* he decided while he watched the boy and his dog disappear around a corner. Sammy thought of his family and wished someone would bring *him* home, too.

The next day, after spending the night in the alley by his old home, Sammy began exploring the nearby streets. He came upon a cat colony close to the foot of the Williamsburg Bridge. There must have been at least a dozen cats living there, some orange, some gray-striped, and one large brown tabby who seemed to be the leader of the group. When Sammy saw the cats gathered around a big pile of fish heads, his stomach growled and he took a few tentative steps towards the cats. *Maybe they'll share with me,* he thought hopefully. But before he could get close, the brown tabby spun around, took a look at Sammy, and hissed menacingly. The rest of the cats started hissing too, and Sammy took off, running as fast as his paws would go, with his tail between his legs.

After several weeks, the lonely toffee-colored dog hadn't had any luck in finding a new, permanent home. Scared of the cats and worried about policemen, Sammy had journeyed across the island of Manhattan, away from his Lower East Side home, in hopes of finding food and shelter. He would occasionally run into other dogs, and sometimes they would share food, but for the most part, the stray dogs of New

York City liked to be on their own. But Sammy didn't! He missed the old apartment, small though it had been. He missed having kids to play with and bones on Sundays. But most of all, he missed having a girl to love him the way Kathleen did.

Eventually Sammy ended up all the way across town, on the West Side of Manhattan near another river. Wearily crawling into a back alley behind a restaurant one night, he found a Sammy-sized space behind a trash can and curled up there. He had never felt so hungry and tired. Before long, a worker came out of the restaurant with a bag of trash. He was a young man of about twenty, and he had warm, friendly brown eyes. The man spotted Sammy.

"Hey, there's a dog back here!" the man exclaimed. Quickly looking behind him and then back to Sammy, he squatted down and scratched Sammy behind the ears, just like Mr.

Moore used to do. Sammy wanted to stand up, but he felt too weak.

"Looks like you're a little down on your luck, huh, buddy? I guess we all are these days." The man shook his head and sighed, looking into the bag of trash he carried. "Well, I wish I could help more, but maybe this'll do you some good." He fished a chicken carcass out of the bag and set it down next to Sammy. Sammy eagerly pounced on it. It was the first meat he'd had in weeks.

"Just don't tell my boss, eh, pal?" the young man laughed, giving Sammy another pat on the head, then heading back inside. The shaggy dog devoured what was left of the chicken, then settled back behind the trash can, resting his tired head on his paws. Sammy fell asleep quickly to dreams of Kathleen, his family, and a happy home.

Chapter Three

The next day, Sammy explored the alleys around the restaurant. He found lots of things: buckets of dishwater, vegetable peelings, and several big, mean, nasty rats. But he didn't find a good place to sleep, food, or a friend. *I guess I could go back to the restaurant*, Sammy thought. *That man might give me more food. But what I really want is someone to take care of me.* He decided that going back to the restaurant was the best thing to do. *At least it's starting to get*

warmer. I hate sleeping outside in the snow.

Sammy arrived at the restaurant alley and began nosing around the trash cans. They must have been emptied recently, he realized with disappointment. Then he heard some voices behind him. Swiveling around eagerly, he looked for the nice man—but only saw two boys.

"Hey look, Augie, it's a stupid ol' stray!" said the bigger of the two boys.

The boy named Augie peered at Sammy and smirked. "Whatta dumb dog. Let's get 'em, Eddie!"

Sammy felt afraid. He watched as the boys started picking up rocks from the ground. Wildly, he looked around for a place to run or hide. He couldn't get past the boys, and the alley turned into a dead end in the other direction. Sammy's only choice was to hide behind the garbage cans. He wedged himself back there as far as he could as the boys began to throw stones at him. One big rock whizzed right past his ear.

"Aw, I missed him," whined Augie.

"It don't matter. We got plenty more of these rocks and he ain't got nowhere to go!" Eddie crowed, aiming a small, pointy stone right at Sammy. The dog's heart was pounding. *Help!* He was afraid to bark—what if someone called the police? Would that be worse? *Why won't the restaurant man come outside?*

Just then, Sammy heard a girl's voice.

"Hey, you jerks, stop throwin' them stones!"

Peering around the trash can, Sammy saw a little girl advancing toward the boys. She was about Kathleen's age, with a mop of red curly hair, a raggedy old sweater over a threadbare dress, and a determined look on her face.

Eddie tossed another stone. It clanged off the side of the can. "We don't take no orders from girls," he scoffed.

"Well, there's a first time for everything," the

girl replied, stomping over to the boys. Sammy watched in bewilderment as the redheaded girl rolled up her sleeves and gave Augie a big push. Augie looked startled; then he turned around and sneered at her.

"So you wanna fight, huh?" Augie dropped his handful of rocks and pushed the girl back.

"Yeah, I wanna fight," she replied. And the three kids were instantly a blur of pushing, shoving, and name-calling. Sammy had seen enough fights on the streets to know that one small girl against two mean boys didn't stand much of a chance. But somehow in a matter of minutes, the girl was standing triumphantly over the boys, who were groaning on the ground.

"Now get outta here, and quit pickin' on dogs, ya hear?" she yelled at Eddie and Augie, who had scrambled to their feet and were limping out of the alley.

Sammy breathed a sigh of relief. The girl approached the trash can and knelt down.

"Hey there, boy. You don't have to be afraid now. Those mean ol' boys are gone," she said kindly. "My name's Annie. And I promise I won't let anyone hurt you."

Can I trust her? Sammy wondered. She did save him from the boys. And she reminded him of Kathleen, with her red hair, good-hearted smile, and friendly voice. So he crept out into the alleyway.

Annie reached out and scratched him behind the ears. "That's a good boy. Let's see. You ain't got no collar. I guess you're on your own, just like me. Maybe we can be on our own together." She gave Sammy a big hug. The dog felt so happy. *Maybe I've found a new owner at last!*

A door slammed from farther down the alley. "Annie!" a woman's voice shrieked. "Get back in here! I got food that needs cooking and a floor that needs mopping. I ain't lettin' you stay here so you can play in the alley." A heavyset blond woman stomped over to where Annie was sitting with Sammy.

Annie stood up. "Mrs. Bixby, look—I found this dog. I think he's a stray. Can I keep him?"

The woman snorted. "Like we ain't givin' you enough, what with your room and board and a good job at the Beanery? You want us to feed a mangy old dog, too? I don't think so."

I'm not *mangy!* Sammy thought indignantly.

"Please?" Annie begged. "I'll share my food with him, and I'll keep him in my room. I'll take care of him. I promise you won't even know he's there."

"Keep a dirty dog in my home? That's the last thing we need around here. I'll call the dogcatcher and have him pick up this mutt. He'll put him to sleep—and then I really won't know he's there," Mrs. Bixby cackled.

Sammy liked sleeping, but it didn't sound like being put to sleep by the dogcatcher was a good thing.

"Please don't do that! I'll work even harder if you let me keep him!" Annie promised.

"You sure will work harder, but you won't be keeping that dog. Now get back inside. We got customers who need their lunch," Mrs. Bixby demanded, and she retreated to the restaurant, slamming the door behind her. *What now?* Sammy wondered.

Annie looked determined. "I won't let the dogcatcher get you! And I won't let Mrs. Bixby get me, either. Not anymore. Let's run away, boy."

Run away? I'm tired of running! But I don't want to be caught by the dogcatcher, either.

"I'll be right back," Annie told Sammy, and she raced inside the restaurant. Everything was happening so fast. In just a minute the redheaded girl was back with a basket. "This is all I've got. Just a little bit of food, a sweater, and not even a penny. But we're free now, boy!" She called to him and they began to run, away from the alley and toward the middle of Manhattan. Sammy hadn't felt this happy since his days of running around with the Moore kids. He trusted the girl with the red curls. *Maybe she will love me just as much as Kathleen did. Maybe I've found my new home at last.*

Chapter Four

After just three blocks, Sammy's newfound happiness was cut short. "Little girl! Come here!" yelled a rough voice. It was a policeman! He was tall and tough looking, and he was swinging a long stick. Annie slowed to a stop, and so did Sammy.

"Yes, sir?" Annie answered the policeman with a sugary voice.

"Ain't that dog a stray? I'm pretty sure I saw him hanging around the garbage cans," the policeman asked.

Sammy looked pleadingly up at Annie. *Don't let him take me!* he thought.

"Oh, he ain't a stray, officer. He's my dog!" Annie replied.

I'm your dog? Sammy thought happily.

"He's your dog, eh?" The policeman didn't look like he believed it. "All right. What's his name?"

"Um . . ." Annie paused. "Sandy! Yeah, his name's Sandy. I call him that because his fur is such a nice sandy color."

Sandy? No, my name is Sammy!

"Sandy, huh? Let's see if he answers to that."

Annie swallowed. "Answer? You want me to call him?"

"That's right," said the officer. "If he's your dog and not a stray, he oughta come when you call him."

Annie sighed and turned to Sammy. "Here, boy! Here, Sandy!" She knelt down and patted her knees gently.

The dog hesitated. His name was Sammy! The Moores had chosen that name for him! But . . . Annie had been so nice to him. After months of being on his own, he really wanted a friend. *And I certainly don't want to go with that policeman. Sandy sounds a lot like Sammy, anyway.* He ran over to Annie and jumped into her arms.

"Good boy!" Annie squealed. "Good boy, Sandy!"

The policeman looked mad. "Well, I suppose maybe he is your dog. But you listen here. You'd better get a leash on him and get him a license, too. If I see you two out here without 'em, he's going to the dog pound. Ya hear? Now get along home."

"Yes, sir," said Annie, still smiling and petting Sandy. As soon as the officer turned a corner, she looked down at the dog.

"Good job, boy. From now on, you're Sandy forever. It's the perfect name for you." She rifled through her basket and shook her head. "I don't know about a license, but I gotta find a leash for you." Annie furrowed her brow, then her eyes lit up.

"I know!" She briskly crossed the street and ran over to a small boy selling newspapers.

"You using that for anything?" Annie asked, pointing to the rough twine that bound a stack of papers.

"Nope. You can have it." The boy shrugged.

"Thanks!" Annie said. She pulled off the twine and trotted back to Sandy, then leaned down to tie it around his neck.

"There," she said, satisfied. "That looks like a collar and a leash. Now, let's get out of here! We ain't too far from Bixby's Beanery and we'd better get going before Mrs. Bixby catches us." The two took off running again.

After about an hour, Annie and Sandy ducked into an alleyway and sat down to rest.

Sandy was worn out, and still scared. *What if we run into another policeman? Or those terrible boys? And where exactly are we going?*

Annie looked at Sandy. "I wish I had somewhere to take you, boy. But the truth is, I'm a runaway. I'm lookin' for my parents, who left me at the orphanage when I was a baby. I was just staying with the Bixbys for some food and shelter for a little while."

Sandy put his head down on his paws and whimpered.

"Don't worry, boy. I'm gonna take care of you. And things will get better. The sun'll come out tomorrow."

Just then, it began to rain.

Annie laughed. "Well, I said tomorrow, didn't I? Come on, Sandy. We gotta find somewhere to sleep tonight."

The two runaways scurried through the streets of New York City, looking for shelter. They passed through Times Square, full of bright neon signs, and kept going until they reached Grand Central Station. "Let's go in here," Annie said. "It'll get us out of the rain." They entered the huge main room of the station, which had a beautiful ceiling painted to look like the stars in the night sky. "Wow, Sandy, ain't it pretty? Someday maybe my parents will take us on a train, to somewhere far away." Sandy liked the sound of that.

Grand Central was full of people carrying bread and meat and sweets home to their families for dinner, and it was making Sandy's stomach growl. Annie noticed and said, "I'm hungry too, boy." She looked around and spotted an apple seller. He looked poor but friendly.

"Hey mister!" Annie called out, walking over to the man. "Where'd you get those apples to sell?"

"At a fruit market," the man replied. "Are you hungry?"

"Well . . ." Annie hesitated.

"Here you go." The man handed Annie two apples. "One for you and one for your dog. No charge."

Sandy's tail wagged eagerly. He gobbled up the apple in just a few bites. "Thank you, sir," Annie said.

"It's my pleasure." The apple seller packed up and headed out of the station. Annie looked thoughtful.

"Sandy, I think we should follow him. He was nice. And we can't stay here all night. the police will probably make us leave."

So the girl and her dog went out again on foot, walking all the way to the East River, where they saw the apple seller enter a small camp. There were several other people there, most of them huddled around fires next to small shacks made out of scraps of tin and wood.

"I don't know what this place is, but it looks

warm," Annie observed. Sandy felt nervous, but he wanted to be out of the cold. They crept down toward the shacks.

A woman looked up from the pot of soup she was tending. "You hungry, little girl?" she asked.

"Oh . . . no," Annie lied. "But my dog, Sandy, is."

The woman smiled and ladled some soup into two empty cans. "Then here's a little something for Sandy. And some extra for you, just in case you change your mind." She winked.

Sandy couldn't believe his luck. In just a short time, Annie had gotten two meals for him! Except . . . yuck, the soup wasn't very good. Still, it was better than nothing.

The apple seller came over.

"Hi, Randy," the soup lady greeted him.

Randy squinted in the dark. "Say, little girl, didn't I just see you at the station? Did you follow me here?"

"Well, sir, I guess we did," said Annie guiltily. "See, I'm lookin' for my parents, and Sandy here is . . . well, I guess he's just lookin' for a home. And we needed a place to sleep, and it was raining, so . . ."

Randy and the soup lady nodded understandingly.

"My name's Sophie, and you can stay with me. Sandy, too," said the woman.

"Gee, thanks! I'm Annie, and we're awful grateful." Sandy wagged his tail. The three of them left Randy and went to make up a bed. Sandy snuggled up with Annie under a pile of newspapers as the rain fell on the shanty's tin roof. It might not have been the most comfortable bed in the world, but Sandy's belly was full and he was safe and dry, so to him, the shanty felt like a palace.

Chapter Five

The next day, Annie and Sandy were awakened by Randy. "Wake up, you two!" he called from outside. Sleepily, the dog followed his new owner out of the shanty, where Randy explained his plan to let Annie help him sell apples.

"We'll split the money," he promised. "I bet having a little girl and a dog around will be a big help to me!"

"It's a deal!" Annie shook his hand firmly and then turned to Sandy. "We can make some money, and ask people about my parents, too." So Annie and Sandy went back to Grand

Central with Randy. Each day, they sold apples, and for every ten apples they sold, Randy would let Annie and Sandy have an apple to eat. "Just to make sure they aren't poisonous," he would say with a sly smile.

Annie asked every person who stopped to buy apples if they had heard of her parents. No one had, but that didn't get her spirits down. Sandy watched all the people leaving and coming back to New York. It made him think of his old family and wonder if they would ever return.

Spring turned into summer, and summer turned into fall. Sandy thought of Kathleen often, but he was getting used to his new life with Annie, and he liked it very much. Apples for lunch, dinner at the shantytown, and Annie as his friend and protector. No more fights with stray dogs or mean boys, no more searching for food on his own, no more lonely nights. But

Annie still hadn't found her parents. When Sandy thought about how much Kathleen loved her own mother and father, it made him very sad that Annie didn't have hers.

On a cold November afternoon, Annie and Sandy were selling apples as usual when Randy ran up to them.

"Annie, get out of here! There's a cop looking for you! He says you're wanted as a runaway orphan!"

The police! Oh, no!

Annie grabbed Sandy by his collar and they ran out of Grand Central Station. The dog's heart pounded as they fled toward the shanty-town. Sophie hid them until Randy arrived.

"You'd better not sell apples anymore, Annie," he said. "The cops are there every day, and now that they know you're a runaway . . ."

Annie sighed. She scratched Sandy's chin. "Maybe with the money I've saved, Sandy and

I can get outta town. Maybe my mother and father left NYC, too. Who knows—they could be in Florida!"

Or California?

But there wasn't any time to make plans. The police showed up at the shantytown.

"Everyone out!" yelled the sergeant. "We're tearin' down this place!"

"But this is our home!" pleaded Sophie.

"Sorry, but I got an order from the judge. Folks that live in those fancy apartments on the East River think this place is a dump. All you bums gotta go."

"They aren't bums! They're good people. And where are they gonna go?" Annie shouted at the cop.

Sandy was trying to hide behind an old piece of ripped cardboard. He still remembered what the boy had said about policemen and dogs.

The cop turned and looked at Annie. His

eyes widened. "Now wait just a minute. Aren't you that runaway orphan? Ain't I seen your picture all over town?"

"No sir! No, I'm, um, her daughter," Annie said, grabbing Sophie's sleeve.

"Oh no you ain't. You're coming with me!" The policeman reached for Annie.

Instinctively, Sandy ran out of his hiding place to defend his protector. He barked at the cop, who just looked down at the dog and laughed.

"I see you got yourself a runaway mutt, too. I'll kill two birds with one stone and take him to the pound."

"Oh no you won't!" Annie kicked the cop in the shin, reached down, and gave Sandy a little push. "Run, boy! Run away!"

Sandy didn't want to. But he knew he had no choice. He ran as quickly as he could, with the officer's shouts ringing in his ears. For a few scary minutes, one of the policemen was right on his tail. But eventually, the dog found himself alone. Sandy slowed and looked behind him. No police. No Randy or Sophie. No Annie.

Chapter Six

Cold and alone, Sandy surveyed his surroundings. He was in an unfamiliar part of town. *Where should I go?* Not back to the alley on the west side, where the mean boys were. He had no idea where Annie might have gone. *Sniff, sniff.* He noticed the smell of the river, so he must not have gone too far west. He padded down a street, following the scent. After a few blocks Sandy came across a familiar sight: the Williamsburg Bridge! He was near the Moores'

old apartment building. Sandy remembered that Kathleen had said they might come back to New York someday. It had been almost a year. He thought happily about the idea of seeing them again. Maybe Kathleen and Annie could even become friends.

It was easy for Sandy to find his old home. Everything looked just the same as he had left it: pushcarts selling food in the streets, children playing, mothers carrying buckets of water and loaves of bread. The Lower East Side was bustling with activity, despite the ragged clothes and dirty faces of many of its occupants. As Sandy turned down the alley, he heard some noisy little boys. His ears perked up. Could it be Michael and Matthew?

But no, it was two unfamiliar boys. One of them, dressed in an overcoat that was too big for him, tossed a ball to the other, who was covered in mud.

"You'd better wash that off before yer

mother gets home," warned the boy in the coat.

As if on cue, a stern-looking woman poked her head down the alleyway.

"Jonah! Have you been playing in the park again? Mrs. Moore left that apartment so clean for us and you are always bringing that *schmutz* into this house. Go find some water and wash yourself off." The woman walked away, muttering.

The little boy named Jonah shrugged and kept tossing the ball.

So I guess the Moores haven't come back after all. At least not here, thought Sandy.

The boy in the overcoat noticed the dog.

"Hey Jonah, look!" he shouted as he bent down to pick up some sticks. Sandy felt hopeful. Michael and Matthew used to play with him by tossing sticks. Maybe these boys would, too?

Jonah looked at Sandy. "I bet he has fleas," he said, wrinkling his nose.

I do not! And you're covered in mud! thought

Sandy, a little hurt. He turned and sprinted out of the alley, away from the boys, the old tenement, and his memories. As night fell, the air got colder, and tiny snowflakes began to fall into Sandy's eyes. He found a quiet spot in a deserted garden and lay down to sleep. Kathleen hadn't come back. Would he ever find Annie again?

Chapter Seven

Sandy decided that the best thing to do would be to stay in the Lower East Side for the time being. At least he knew the neighborhood, and the rest of Manhattan didn't seem to be much better. Well, except for the shantytown, but he couldn't go back there now. The police had probably torn it down, anyway. So he began to explore his old haunts. The butcher remembered him and tossed him a bone. There was hardly any meat on it, but Sandy chewed on it greedily. He passed Kathleen's old school and a teacher gave him an apple, which made him think of Annie. All of the signs of life were there on the Lower East Side, but Sandy could tell that things were still going poorly for New Yorkers. Food was scarce, the children were skinny, and the adults often looked tired and scared. Sandy understood. He felt the same way.

After heading slightly north to St. Mark's Place one afternoon, Sandy came across a building he'd never seen before. It was a two-story building with a sign that said "New York City Municipal Orphanage." *Orphanage*, thought Sandy. *Annie said she ran away from an orphanage.*

Several small girls were in the front yard, shoveling snow. The smallest one was struggling with her shovel.

"Come on, Molly, you gotta go faster than that! Miss Hannigan said we gotta have the sidewalk shoveled by lunchtime," the biggest girl said.

"Aw, leave her alone, Pepper. Lunch is only going to be a bologna sandwich. Same as it is every day," said another orphan.

A bologna sandwich sounded pretty good to Sandy!

"Yeah, well, I don't want to miss out on a sandwich 'cause Molly here can't handle her shovel," retorted Pepper.

"Oh, my goodness!" murmured a nervous-looking girl.

"I miss Annie," sighed little Molly.

Annie??

Sandy crept closer to the girls.

"Oh, my goodness, I miss her too," the nervous orphan agreed.

Pepper rolled her eyes. "You too, Tessie? Fine. Give me your shovel, Molly. You and Tessie and July can go cry over your precious Annie. But this means I get half of your sandwich."

Sandy thought for a moment. The big girl, Pepper, didn't seem very friendly, but the others did. And they were orphans who knew a girl named Annie. Even if she wasn't here, maybe they could take care of him for a little while. He padded slowly over to the smallest girl.

Molly turned after giving her shovel to Pepper and spotted the shaggy brown dog. "Puppy!" she squealed, and bent down to hug him.

The orphan named July ran over. She studied Sandy carefully, then reached down and petted his head. "He seems sweet, all right. Not like some of the strays we usually see around here."

"Oh, my goodness, oh, my goodness!" exclaimed Tessie.

"His coat's all matted and he's real skinny. Guess you have a hard-knock life too, huh?" July observed.

Sandy wished he could ask them about Annie!

"Hey, what's all this?" Pepper asked, walking over with another orphan. "Oh, no," she said, spotting Sandy. "You better get that dog outta here before—"

The front door opened and slammed.

A mean-looking woman in a floral dress and a long sweater stormed out of the orphanage. Her face was scrunched up into a grimace.

"Just what are you rotten orphans up to? I'm tryin' to get some sleep, here."

The girls looked guiltily at one another. Pepper stepped forward. "Molly found a dog, Miss Hannigan."

"Can we . . . can we keep him?" July asked bravely.

Miss Hannigan walked over to the girls, slowly and calmly. Sandy trembled. She glared down at him.

"A dog? A DOG? I got enough dirt in the place thanks to you lousy kids. No, you can't keep him. This is a place for stray kids, not stray dogs." And with that, Miss Hannigan grabbed Sammy roughly by his rope collar. Tessie whimpered and July shouted in protest.

"That's enough out of all of you!" Miss

Hannigan shouted. "Now get back to work. I'll take this mutt and put him where he really belongs—the pound!"

Sandy tried to pull away, but Miss Hannigan's grip was too strong. He could hear the little girls' cries behind him as the mean woman dragged him into the orphanage.

Chapter Eight

Sandy struggled as Miss Hannigan used the rope around his neck to tie him to a chair. She then stepped over to a desk and began to look through a pile of papers. Sandy tried to pull away, but Miss Hannigan had tied the knot too tightly.

"Let's see, I know I have that number somewhere . . . aha! Here it is." She dialed the phone.

"Hello, I'm at the orphanage on St. Mark's, and I've got a dog that needs . . . taking care of. Yes, thank you. As soon as possible. You say your man is nearby? Good."

She hung up and slumped down into a chair.

"I swear, these kids are gonna be the end of me," Miss Hannigan muttered to herself. "First that darn Annie runs away. A police officer brings her back."

So Annie had gotten caught!

Miss Hannigan sighed. "And then, she ain't here half a day before she gets taken to spend Christmas with Oliver Warbucks, of all people. The richest man in the world! She don't deserve it."

Sandy's thoughts raced. So Annie had been taken back to the orphanage, and then rescued by a rich man? The dog was glad that Annie was safe, but he was also a little sad that he'd found Annie's orphanage only to just miss her.

Miss Hannigan put her head on the table and fell asleep within minutes. She began to snore.

A clock on the wall ticked. Fifteen minutes. Half an hour. Sandy wondered how long he would be there.

But he didn't have much time to think about that. The dogcatcher had shown up at the orphanage.

After a rough ride in the back of an uncomfortable truck, Sandy was yanked by his collar into a windowless, musty building. As his eyes adjusted to the darkness, Sandy began to pick up on the smell of other dogs as he was led down into a basement. The dogcatcher shoved him into a small, cramped cage and locked it.

"Be back for you later," the dogcatcher joked meanly, and left. Sandy listened to the sound of his footsteps retreating up the stairs. He looked around. There were a few other dogs in cages all around him. A small gray poodle with a matted coat cowered in the corner of her cage. A big, shaggy old black mutt was sleeping. A friendly looking pit bull paced his cage. None of the dogs looked happy.

Sandy thought back to the things he'd heard about the dog pound.

What would happen if a policeman caught you? You'd go straight to the dog pound and I'd never see you again, that's what.

I'll call the dogcatcher and have him pick up this mutt. He'll put him to sleep—and then I really won't know he's there.

Sandy gulped. He didn't have a very good feeling about being at the pound.

Several days passed. Sandy and the other dogs were given water but very little food. Then one morning, Sandy woke up groggily to the sound of the poodle howling. Sandy had been sleeping off and on through the night, finding it hard to get comfortable on the cold cement floor. He didn't know quite what was in store for him, but he knew it wasn't good. He thought of Annie and the other nice orphans. He wished desperately to have a friend again who would brush his fur and feed him treats.

The sound of footsteps echoed down the stairs. The dogs all woke up and began to bark nervously, expecting the dogcatcher.

But Sandy heard a woman's voice instead.

"I truly hope that the dog is still here, or my employer will want to have a word with your supervisor."

The woman came into view. She was young, slim, and very well dressed. She daintily raised a gloved hand to her nose as she walked down the line of cages.

The dogcatcher shuffled behind her. "Uh, lady, I'm just doin' my job here. But you can have a look. No one else wants these mutts, that's for sure."

That's not true! Annie wants me! Sandy wanted to say.

"You may call me Miss Farrell," the lady replied primly as she peeked into each cage as she passed. "A poodle . . . a pit bull . . . no, no. Don't you have— Oh!"

Miss Farrell had stopped in front of Sandy's cage. She scrutinized him and looked down at a sheet of paper.

"Shaggy coat. Sandy color. Mixed breed. Hmm. Yes, I think this is the one." She nodded at the dogcatcher, who pulled out a ring of keys.

"He's all yours, then," the man shrugged as he opened Sandy's cage.

Freedom! Sandy eagerly ran out of his cage and shook himself. Miss Farrell petted him on the head.

"Would you please take that dirty rope off his neck?" she asked the man nicely but firmly. The man grunted in reply and pulled off the piece of twine that Annie had used as Sandy's collar. The pretty lady reached down and clipped a brand-new collar and leash around his neck.

"Yes, I think you must be Sandy," she said softly.

Wait . . . how does she know my name?

Miss Farrell began to lead Sandy to the stairs, then paused.

"What will happen to the rest of these dogs?" she asked.

"You don't want to know," the dogcatcher said with a smirk.

Miss Farrell narrowed her eyes. "I'd like to make a phone call, please," she said politely.

The dogcatcher rolled his eyes. "Yes, your highness. Up the stairs."

The lady handed Sandy's leash to him. "Thank you. I'll be right back."

In a matter of minutes, Miss Farrell returned.

"You're not to touch any of these other dogs. My employer will find homes for them," she instructed.

"But they're all scheduled to be put to sleep today!" the dogcatcher protested.

"You do know who my employer is, yes?" she inquired sweetly. "We'll have someone coming by later to pick them all up."

"Fine," grumbled the man.

And with that, Sandy followed his new savior out of the pound and back into the light.

Chapter Nine

Miss Farrell led Sandy to a big, shiny black limousine. After helping the dog into the back seat and settling herself next to him, she said to the driver, "Back to the mansion, please." The limousine pulled away and Sandy stuck his nose out of the car window. He watched in wonder as they sped away from the dog pound over to Fifth Avenue. As the street numbers got higher, the apartments and buildings got fancier and fancier. Sandy had never seen such nice places. Finally, the limousine stopped at Fifth Avenue and 82nd Street, in front of a huge marble mansion. Miss Farrell opened the door and led Sandy up the front steps. A tall man in a green uniform opened the door.

"Hello, Drake!" said Miss Farrell brightly.

Drake looked down his nose at Sandy and frowned.

"Oh, dear. This . . . this is the dog?" he said dubiously.

"Yes, I'm quite certain it is. As you can see, we'll need to give him a bath, a haircut, some grooming . . . well, everything, I suppose."

"Indeed. I've already called in an excellent groomer. He's in the sixth bathroom in the right wing of the second floor."

As Sandy followed Drake and Miss Farrell, he looked up at the ceiling of the foyer. This was definitely the biggest room he'd been in since Grand Central Station. The dog had no idea why he had been brought to this place, or why Miss Farrell knew his name, but it was certainly a million times nicer than the streets or the pound, and a bath sounded very good to him. The hallways of the mansion were lined with statues, paintings, and expensive-looking carpets. Sandy felt somewhat ashamed to be putting his dirty paws on such nice things. Miss Farrell must have noticed his tail between his legs, because she said, "Don't worry, Sandy. We have the best cleaning staff in New York City. We have more maids than the mayor! And we'll get you cleaned up in no time."

In the bathroom, a short, pleasant man introduced himself as the groomer. He dunked Sandy in an enormous marble bathtub full of warm water and lavender-scented soap. Bubbles flew in the air as the groomer scrubbed the dog's shaggy fur vigorously. Next, he rubbed Sandy down with a soft, fluffy towel. When Sandy's coat was dry, the groomer set about clipping Sandy's nails, cutting and grooming his fur, and fastening his new red collar around his neck.

"All done, boy! I bet that feels pretty good, doesn't it?"

It sure did. Sandy felt better than good. He felt relaxed and safe. But he still wasn't sure what he was doing in this wonderful place, and why everyone was being so nice to him. With the exception of the Moores, Randy, and Sophie, grown-ups didn't usually treat him very well.

Miss Farrell, who had been observing, nodded in satisfaction. "Yes, he looks wonderful. If you would, please take him down to the small mudroom off the kitchen downstairs. He can have a few days of rest before the big Christmas party."

Was it Christmastime already? Sandy remembered how the Moores used to celebrate with presents. They were always so happy, even though the presents were small. And Kathleen would always slip him some of the Christmas turkey. *Maybe they'll have turkey here*, Sandy thought hopefully.

In the next few days, Sandy had lots of rest on big, fluffy pillows and as many meals of delicious meat as he wanted. *I think I'm gonna like it here!*

On Christmas morning, a young maid not much older than Annie approached Sandy with a large box. "Don't be scared, now, Sandy," she reassured him. "You'll only be in this for a few minutes."

Sandy wanted to believe her, but being in the box made him think of the cage at the dog pound, and he didn't like it at all. He felt himself being carried a short way and then set down.

"I've got one more present for you," said a man's muffled voice.

Someone took off the top of Sandy's box and peered in. Sandy looked up and saw . . . Annie! He barked excitedly.

"Sandy! It's my Sandy!" Annie shrieked happily. Sandy leaped out of the box and jumped on Annie, putting his paws on her shoulders and licking her face. Annie hugged him tightly. "Oh, Sandy, I thought I'd never see you again."

Me, either, thought Sandy.

Annie turned to a tall, bald man standing next to her. "Oh, Daddy, thank you so much." He smiled.

Daddy? Did Annie find her parents?

"I have so much to tell you, Sandy," Annie said, hugging him again. "Turns out, my real parents died a long time ago. But Mr. Warbucks here, he's going to adopt me. He's just about the best person I know. Well, I know that for sure, now that he brought you to me. Now we won't ever be apart." Sandy nuzzled into her arms.

Miss Farrell walked over to the girl and her dog. "We have another surprise, Annie," she said, smiling. Just then, Sandy noticed that there were more people in the room—lots more. Including all of the orphans that he'd met at

Miss Hannigan's! Little Molly ran over to give him a hug.

"Do you like dogs, too, Molly?" Miss Farrell asked.

"Yes!" Molly squealed.

"We all do," July chimed in.

"Then I have some good news. There were several other dogs at the pound who needed saving, and all of your new families are happy to take them with you. One per child. That is, if you'd like a pet."

"Oh, my goodness, oh, my goodness!" Tessie cried happily. Even Pepper looked excited.

So the other orphans found new parents, too, thought Sandy. *How wonderful!*

Drake opened a door to yet another room in the cavernous mansion, and all of the dogs Sandy remembered from the pound came bounding out. The little poodle now sported pink bows, and it ran right over to Molly.

July petted the big black dog, whose fur was now soft and shiny. And Pepper began playing catch with the pit bull, who romped around so joyfully that the servants grabbed the vases and candlesticks to keep them steady. Sandy was so relieved that the other dogs had been saved, too! He took in the scene around him. He saw the orphans—that is, the *former* orphans—playing and opening presents. He smelled Christmas turkey *and* roast beef wafting through the air. Holiday songs played on a gramophone. It was the best day of Sandy's life. And he knew that Kathleen would be very happy if she knew.

Annie smiled up at Mr. Warbucks and then down at Sandy. "All I ever wanted was a family. This wasn't exactly what I thought I'd find when I went looking, but I sure am glad I did find it. I don't need anything but you. Both of you!"

Mr. Warbucks blushed and gave her a hug.

"C'mon, Sandy, let's go look at the snow!"

Annie and Sandy ran to the big picture

window overlooking Fifth Avenue. The whole street was covered in a beautiful white blanket of snow. The sun shone down over the sparkling city. "Look, Sandy, it's just like I told you," Annie said, squeezing the shaggy dog. "The sun came out. Tomorrow is here."

Yes, thought Sandy happily. *Yes, it is*.

For more information about Annie— including fun games and activities—please visit www.thirteen.org/annie